THE SOUL OF ANNE GRANGER

ANUSHKA GUPTA

Made with ♥ on the Notion Press Platform
www.notionpress.com

I wanted to write this book because I love reading horror and want other's also to read it.

Contents

Contents

Foreword

Main Characters:

Bob Bradley:

Age – 14
    Class – 9
    Weakness – He is very lazy
    and very fraidy boy
    Strength – He is very good at drawing
    Alex William:
    Age – 14
    Class – 9
    Weakness – He is very weird
    Strength – He is very good at cyber things
    Fred Wesley:
    Age – 14
    Class – 9
    Weakness – He is a food addict
    Strength – He has nice humor
    Ginny Bradley:
    Age – 34
    Occupation – Teacher
    Weakness – She is a phone addict
    Strength – She loves to read
    Anne Granger:
    Age – 32 (dead)
    Occupation – Was a Software Engineer
    Weakness – Was very emotional

Strength – Was great violinist
Ruby Granger:
Age - 12 (dead)
Student
Weakness - Was very emotional
Strength - Was very smart

Preface

The book is about three friends who get lost and spend days in a haunted house where they met some spirits, etc. A spirit name Anne is wandering there in search of the killer of her daughtrer.

Prologue

Bob and his two friends, Alex and Fred, have lost their way back from home. It was nighttime. They decided to stay in a place that looked like an ordinary house. Is the house safe or not? Read with me what happened to all three friends. Are they safe or not?

Acknowledgements

Many thanks to the people who helped me during writing this book.
my friends and family huge thanks to them.

xiii

CHAPTER ONE

WAKE UP!

October 29, 2022, Saturday

One sizzling dawn. I woke up from my mom yelling wake up, wake up. It's already 8:00 AM. Then I whispered (It's just 8:00, she and dad wake up early. it doesn't designate late anyhow, and no one hears me). I spoke. I am reaching mom. When I bolted from the mattress, I stabbed my leg on the sharpness of the bed. I said That hurts.

Then I walked with my leg in the air for 2 minutes. I squeaked not again. That hurts. I stubbed my exact leg with Alcazar* (Alcazar - a Spanish castle). My mom yelled again. What happened? I said frivolity, nothing mom, She voiced ok. Now go fast, brush, cleanse and have your breakfast.

CHAPTER TWO

CATASTROPHES!

(entering the lavatory) I was sleepy. I didn't see the soap fibbing on the floor and strode on it. Damn! That hurts. Ahh! I forgot to familiarize myself. My name is Bob Bradley. (He has a convention. Acquaint himself with every person) My mother's name is Ginny Bradley.

Where was I? Yeah, I reminisce. I was stumbling on the soap. (slipping continues) I smacked my head on the wash basin and fell off. A needle hit me right into my bum. I hopped and hopped after leaping into the bathtub. The bathtub has superheated water.

I didn't know and vaulted into it. I turned red as a chili. I picked out the needle from my tramp. I unlocked the bathtub faucet as regular water and plunged my noggin into it.

Finally! what an alleviation. I said (in a low voice) I hate mom. She loves to take hot water baths. She didn't realize this time.

Mom forgot to take out the water.

Then I took solace in bathing. I relished it the first time. I got prepared and headed for breakfast.

CHAPTER THREE

BREAKFAST

(On the dining tableland) My mom permitted me my breakfast. I said, mom. What is this? She said, What ensued? I said, how can you offer bananas and eggs? She says why? I said bananas and eggs are bizarre and inimitable. She thwarted me and said block it. First, endeavor it.

I spoke ok, but internally my intellect was speaking no, don't swallow it. I have no choice. I have to ingest it. After endeavoring it out, yum! It's incredible.

My mom: see, I advised you.

Me: Yea, I agree

CHAPTER FOUR

PLAY OUTDOORS!

(11:00 AM) I was eyeing the TV. Mom came into the aisle. She shrieked. Switch off the television. Go outdoors. Did I say why? (I am scared of my mom. She can be too rigorous sometimes).

She said, how dare you cross-questioned me? I said no, mom, I didn't mean. She said to stop providing justifications. I am saying, for your fitness.

I said I am going. Mom responded That's like a fine chap.

CHAPTER FIVE

OUTDOORS

(In the park) I contacted my friends Alex and Fred. They said to arrive in 2 minutes. I responded ok. (Alex and Fred came)

I said Hi. Fred said Hi (arrogantly). I asked, what happened? Why are you talking so arrogantly? Alex said nothing but Fred was a little upset. Fred nodded. I said ok, but why was he upset?

Fred answered. I got scolded by my dad for getting bad grades in exams. I said, don't worry it will be fine.

(Talking for some time) We decided to go home now

CHAPTER SIX

AT DINNER!

(At dinner tableland) I was in the chamber playing video games. My mom requested me to reach out for dinner 2-3 times. I didn't. She yelled, arrive right now. I understood some things were about to be a cataclysm. I came quickly into the kitchen.

She said I informed you to come for dinner 2-3 times. Why don't you come for dinner? I responded to Mom. I was doing something. Mom said, what? Were you playing video frolicking's? I replied Umm, Yes, Mom.

Mom said now you will get retribution. I reply, why, mom? Mom spoke, for not hearing me.

For not hearing me. Mom said your penalty is that you can't play video games for one week. I said What? Mom declared yes, directly go and have dinner. I was despairing, but I responded ok.

(At dining tableland) Mom served me the food. I ingested it when I was going to hand my plate to my mom. I accidentally slipped it. Mom heard it and asked you to drop the receptacle? I said Sorry, mom, I accidentally dropped it. Mom said now I am accidentally increasing your retribution. Your punishment is extended for one more week. Now, go to your enclosure and shuteye.

CHAPTER SEVEN

BEDTIME!

(on my bed) I was scrutinizing the phone. Abruptly, My mom opened the doorway. I quickly lowered the phone and picked up the book next to me. I was pretending that I was reading a book. She questioned what I was doing? I responded I am reading, mom.

She said, Wow! You are reading an opposing book.

I checked and said, sorry, mom, I was looking at my phone. You will have retribution. Your penalty is you will have to scour the store room at dusk. I questioned, Why night? (I am scared of the dark and our store room has no glare.)

She replied I have a stagnant schedule for you hereafter. I whispered

(why are you eradicating my Sunday?) She said did you say anything? I said no, mom. Mom switches off the sunlight and goes to her room. I went to slumber.

(thinking about my hard-to-fast timetable.)

CHAPTER EIGHT

Peep-Peep

30, October 2022, Sunday
,7:30 AM

It was a delightful morning till the alarm clock didn't wake me up. I switched off my alarm clock and woke up. I saw the clock, and it was just 7:30 AM. I was like, what the perdition? Mom set the alarm for 7:30.

Mom squeaked You are, awakened, nice. She wished me a cheerful Halloween. I said, what, i-it-it's hall-Halloween? (I stammered) She said, yea, I have a ton of work for you.

I thought she would have to three-four jobs. Mom said your schedule is on the fridge. I said ok. She asked first to go to the bath and then study it.

CHAPTER NINE

SURPRISE!

(Doorbell rings) I was heading to the lavatory, and the sudden doorbell tingled. I went to unlock the door. I was astounded to see who it was. It was my sister Angelina Bradley. She is my cousin's sister. Mom anointed her, nicknamed an angel. It's contrary to what she is. I think angel is a jeopardy maker! She dissembles to be good. In front of everyone, but if no adult is there. She would be a cataclysm. She is 10.

Angel said Hi. It doesn't seem that you are happy enough to see me. I said no, I am cheerful, but I was not. Mom came to see who it was. (When the angel saw mom.) She embraced mom and said to the aunt. I am so delighted to see you. Mom said I am also glad to see you.

I asked mom. Where is the angel going to sleep? (I asked because I didn't want to share my room.) Mom said She's going to stay in your room. Angel said, ok, aunt. I whispered no. Angel said to the aunt. I am going to bathe. Mom said ok, dear. I said, what, no. I am going to the lavatory first. Mom said to let her bathroom first. (Angel headed to the bathroom.)

CHAPTER TEN

FURTHERMORE, A SURPRISE!

Angel gave me a wicked smile. Then left for the bathroom. I knew

From now forward, I have been more prudent. When she came out of the bathroom, she called me and said, now, You can bathe.

I went to the bathroom. I brushed my teeth and took some reassurance. (I took it easy because my toothbrush was ok.)

Then I took a shower. (After taking a shower. I recognized That my skin was all pink.) I yelled. Angel laughed. I cleaned myself from the tap water. I knew I decided. to take vengeance on the angel.

Angel said how you enjoyed my surprise. I said It was horrendous.

I will take my payback.

CHAPTER ELEVEN

BACKFIRED!

(At breakfast table) I sneaked into the kitchen. I can take payback. Mom was in the temple. Angel was watching tv. I decided to go to the kitchen. I went to the kitchen.

I put a spicy sauce in one hot dog and put ketchup in one. I went to the hall where I could pretend I was watching tv.

Mom called out to Bob and Angel dear, come for breakfast.

Angel came first and mom served one hotdog for the angel. She called Bob to come fast. When I came, I saw an angel happily eating a hotdog happily. I almost fainted because I knew! I got the spicy hotdog.

Mom said bob what are you waiting for? eat the hotdog bob. I ate it was so spicy that I drank two water bottles. I whispered my plan got backfired. I saw angel laughing.

CHAPTER TWELVE

SLUMBER!

(at 10:00 PM.)

I was watching tv. Mom was inspecting notebooks. Angel was reading books (She adores reading books.) Mom screeched, "kids to go to sleep" Angel replied ok, my dearest aunt. Mom said very pleasingly, darling. I said, mom, I am also heading to rest. Mom spoke ok.

(Mom is biased toward the angel. Once we had a horrible fight, The reason was kind of lame. I stepped on the angel's leg by mistake. Angel hit me hard enough that I thought I was going to a coma. Mom said you must have done something.)

I lay down on the bed and went to slumber.

Goodnight!

CHAPTER THIRTEEN

SCARY MORNING!

31st, October

2022, Monday

I woke up at 8:00 AM (I know it's early). When I flared my eyes, I fainted for a moment. It was a dreadful demon standing in front of my eyes.

When I fanned my eyes again, I saw angel, chortling and chuckling. Angel said you are so coward. I said, I am not a coward. Why did you terrified me?

Angel said because it's Halloween you, ignoramus. I said what?

(I hate Halloween. I am frightened of them.)

CHAPTER FOURTEEN

NOT AGAIN!

(After bathing) I went to the breakfast table. Angel was devouring her breakfast. I saw my breakfast. I said, Monster Monster!

Angel burst out giggling.

Mom screeched,

What happened, bob?

Angel replied nothing, my beloved aunt. I drew a funny monster face in his breakfast.

He is even fearful of that. Mom replied,

He is a weakling(No one gave me an opportunity to talk.)

Angel gave a wicked smile. I left then

CHAPTER FIFTEEN

PARK!

(12:01 PM) Mom said to me & angel.

"You should go for the garden walk. Angel replied ok, aunt. I said why? (I whispered I don't want to go to the park.) Mom said you both have to go to the park. You don't have any choices.

(we went to the park) After a while, I was wondering, and angel was playing. Angel came to me and started crying. (She was acting.) I asked her why she was crying. She said just wanted to see you punished.

(angel ran towards the abode.) I ran after her to stop her. When mom saw her, she said furiously what happened and why she was crying? she said aunt bob hit me extremely painful. I said no, mom, she is fibbing. Mom said no, you must have done something otherwise, she would not cry.

Angel said yes, aunt. Mom said (looking towards me) you will get a punishment. your punishment is you have to scour the storeroom right now. I said please no.

Angel gave me a vicious smile. I left for cleaning.

CHAPTER SIXTEEN

CRYSTAL BALL

(In the storeroom) I had a torch and a broom.

All of a sudden, the door of the closet got locked,

I was just about to cry and said, "who the bloody hell" and slammed the door.

I started cleaning with the help of my torch.

After cleaning for a while, I saw something which was glowing

It was underneath the large filthy parcel,

I somehow managed to yanked that box and took that enigmatic glowing thing in my hand,

It was like a crystal orb.

It somehow hypnotized me, the lovely sound of a woman singing was coming from that ball.

All of a sudden a beam of white light came through that ball and took me inside the ball.

It was like I was on our planet.

(Now the absolute thrill starts.)

CHAPTER SEVENTEEN

FORAGING FOR A PLACE

It was a sweltering night. I was hanging out with my friends in an automobile and we mislaid our way. I forgot to familiarize myself. My name is Bob Bradley. My buddies' names are Alex and Fred. Where was I?

I'm bumfuzzled.

I recall. I was gabbing about how we misplaced our boardwalk.

My and Alex's phone batteries departed. Fred, as expected, shirked to fetch his phone. Then we decided to scrutinize a home or location for the nighttime. After stepping for a period, we caught a house.

It was glimpsing like an ordinary place, Conversing for a while. We ultimately selected to stay in the house because we had no alternative.

When we glanced upwards at the sky. we saw the temperature was overshadowed and rainy.

There can be a gale at any juncture. Hauling out luggage, we went inside the house.

We foraged for the controller desperately because we were all terrorized by the gloaming.

Spooky commotions were arriving from a compartment in the Only then, I ceased and said That hurts. I screeched. Alex strolled on my foot. Alex sounded sorry. I bounced like a rabbit and magically pushed the controller.

Alex and Fred said pleasingly; well done. I said Thanks (I didn't have any intention, it occurred magically). Currently, I ameliorated that there was no darkness in the aisle.

I peeked on my left side, the top, and then on the right side. I essentially fainted from what I had witnessed.

There was a shadow. It was a female's shadow, her nails were very prolonged, and her hair also, I assume, was a sorceress.

My friends chuckled and giggled so extensively. that Fred almost cried from chuckling. I said stop it, buddies. I am not fibbing.

They said, ``Are you absurd? I said, please acknowledge me. (I knew no one would believe me.)There was a cock. I mean, clock Alex giggled for 2 minutes continually. Fred chuckled after him.

I hollered. Why are you laughing? I didn't reveal a joke. It was solely a misstep of the tongue.

Alex's voice was frivolity. I recalled a prank. Fred said I was chuckling because I glimpsed Alex giggling.

I said, skimming at the timepiece. It's 10 o'clock. Let's examine the chamber and slumber. Alex and Fred swapped their eyes and spoke ok (concurrently).

CHAPTER EIGHTEEN

ANOTHER DAY!

At 6:00 AM.

I woke up to a bizarre sound.

It was a dreadful sound.

I got frightened that I ran as fast as I could to call my friends so that we could go home.

I ran and I felt someone was following me.

(In Fred and Alex's room) When I told them what I heard they chortled very hard. They were not acknowledging me.

I was trying to persuade them.

They were not listening to me.

Alex said if you think there's an apparition in this house,

Let's just stay here for one more day and prove that there's no ghoul or spirit over here.

Fred acquiesced to what Alex said.

I said are you guys infuriated but, unfortunately, I could not leave them alone because they are my companions.

(After all of us had taken a bath.)

Fred said he was famished. I said I was also ravenous.

We all decided to go to the kitchen of this house and make something for us to eat.

(In the kitchen)

Alex saw some cereal in a bowl so he said he would have that cereal. I and Fred were scouring for food. after a while, Fred found two eggs in a basket,

Me and Fred took one each and cooked omelets for both of us.

In my omelet, I saw a countenance of a lady wailing. I immediately shouted. Alex and Fred were shocked to see me shouting.

They asked me what happened.

Why was I shouting?

I replied that I saw a countenance of a female crying in my omelet.

Fred said now I am getting outlandish and

Alex agreed with him.

I was enraged at them, I said I was not crazy

you guys will concede they're a ghost in this house.

(In the afternoon) There's no f**k**g ghost in this house.

Immediately someone compelled him damn hard. He was about to fall from the stairs.

Now, He started to believe there was a ghost in this house. He apologized to the ghost for his behavior. Alex still does not believe in ghosts.

He said there's no ghost. I asked him then who pushed Fred.

He said maybe his leg got imbalanced and he fell. Fred argued his leg was not balanced and someone pushed him.

(Watching TV) We all were watching a show.

All of sudden, the light goes off.

Me and Fred got scared the TV was still going on.

Alex said there was no need to worry.

It may be a glitch.

Me and Fred said let's go home, the area was not safe.

Alex, was not agreeing with it.

We have to stay in that house for the whole day.

(dinner) We all were having our dinner,

Fred said he was not getting a good vibe right now.

We all continued to have dinner. Suddenly the wind started blowing very fast. A plate on the table fell and cracked.

I said maybe it was because of the wind.

Alex and Fred agreed with me.

(I said that to calm myself that there's no ghost close to us right now.)

CHAPTER NINETEEN

THE STRANGE SOUND

(At night at 3 AM.) I heard a peculiar., mysterious noise. The sound was as if a woman was wailing very inadequately.

she was in misery.

I called out to my friends and they said they could not hear any sound and said my ears were ringing.

After a while, They also realized that a sound was coming from somewhere.

Fred hears a mouse sound.

Alex hears the same sound as mine.

Alex said it was just counterfeit.

Fred was unnerved like me.

Alex said there's nothing to be scared of, let's sleep.

I somehow persuaded Alex to let's go and check it.

We all went to check the bizarre sound.

CHAPTER TWENTY

THE SOUL OR SOULS

(roaming in the hall.) As we moved ahead, the sound got more potent and more potent.

In front of us, there was a strange-looking door

blood driblets was on the door.

We all were skittish.

We all went inside the door.

My voice clogged.

The entire chamber was red.

I was like blood everywhere.

We all heard a female voice saying salutation to us.

The wind started fast female was levitating in the sky.

The female was ravishing.

She was crying.

Alex screamed after seeing her, Fred almost fainted. The female said them no need to be fearful. The female also said her name was Anne Granger.

I said are you going to impair us? Anne replied relax I am not going to harm you all. she needed our help. Fred asked if you are not going to harm us then why you cracked the plate plagued us.

Anne said we all need to be prudent it's not only her soul in this house there are other souls also which was bugging us.

I asked, can we leave the house.

Anne said you all has entered the house now,

you all can not go without doing my work.

Fred asked what, is your work?
Anne begins to wail.
Alex said why, are you crying.
She replied she had a daughter whose name was ruby granger.
Ruby, was murdered.
In dissecting her daughter's case
She, was also murdered.
She wants to kill her and her daughter's murderer.
We all felt sorry for her and her daughter.
We wanted to help her.
She wiped her incisions and said your expedition not be easy,
You all will have to face many challenges!
Large number of souls and dark mysticism will come your way.
You all can even die in this journey.
We all were scared, we still agreed to help her.
She was full of bliss and thanked us.

CHAPTER TWENTY-ONE

THE SOULS IN OUR WAY

(In one bedroom) Me, Alex, and Fred was brooding about what to do now.

Fred said let's just back out.

Fred said we should flee from here.

I replied we should not cease

I said we should oblige her.

Alex said I was right.

Alex said we have to make a strategy.

(Anne was in the room.)

Anne said the first step, you all have to find a golden locket.

I asked where we would find the golden locket.

Anne replied it would be in a secret room in this house.

Anne said she would help us perpetrate to the room.

Fred said why?

I said Fred, don't be so desirous.

Fred said ok, sorry.

Anne said first, you have to find the secret door which will not be easy for you will have to create a visibility elixir.

(visibility position only we can see the invisible door.)

Alex asked how we could make a visibility potion.

Anne said you would need:

1) A hair strand of any brown-haired boy.

2) A pumpkin slice

3) The blood of a boy whose skin is the fairest and his blood of his should be ebony.

Fred said first is easy.

He could give his hair strands.

I said the second one was easy

They could easily take a pumpkin from the kitchen and cut it.

Alex said what about the third one?

Fred said who is the fairest of all of us?

(Fred and Alex both gape at me.)

I said guys stop staring at me.

I agree I am the fairest from all of us.

What about black blood,

I don't have it.

(Anne looks melancholy.)

Fred said, have you ever seen your blood?

I replied, no and said I am a normal human like everybody.

so, how come I will have black blood?

Alex said I was right, how come I will have black blood.

I said maybe we will never be able to find a person with black blood.

suddenly Anne remembered something she said one of you surely has black blood otherwise you all wouldn't be able to enter this palace.

Alex asked but how come we will be able to figure out who has the black blood? (everyone thought for a while)

Anne said you all will find a magical knife in the cupboard and you have to cut your skin through that knife but there's one problem: the knife could take your soul also if your soul is not pure so be careful.

We all agreed to take the risk. We opened the cupboard and I took the knife.

That knife was glowing like diamonds were embedded in the knife. I scratched my skin with the knife. I screamed as hard as I could. It was painful.

I was shocked to see my blood was black. Alex and Fred almost fainted to see what was happening. Anne was happy to see black blood tears of hope lit in her eyes. She immediately collected my blood drops in a container.

She asked Fred to bring pumpkin slices from the kitchen. Fred brought it.

Then she asked Alex to bring the cauldron near the bed.

She took a strand of Fred's hair and put it in the cauldron then she put the slice of pumpkin inside the cauldron and last but not least she put some drops of my blood.

She asked me to mix it because my soul was pure. I mixed it. After a while of mixing a beam of light came shearing the cauldron inside it was a potion, the potion of visibility.

CHAPTER TWENTY-TWO

GOLDEN LOCKET

We all immediately drank the potion.

The experience was like a boastful energy entering our bodies, after a second or so, we felt ordinary. We asked Anne what to do now.

She replied now you all would be able to see the invisible entrance.

(We searched the whole cottage for 1-2 hours, searching for the invisible door.)

At 6:48 PM we finally found it. We were all full of joy.

(we went inside the room.)

In the center, there was the golden locket in a transparent chest.

lasers were patrolling the box, we have to get that locket so that we can see the countenance and location of the person who murdered ruby.

Alex asked how we were supposed to take the golden locket.

I said, we have to pass the lasers to get the golden locket.

Fred was an expert at passing the lasers, he said he would pass the lasers and get the locket.

We agreed with Fred. (Fred passed the lasers and brought the locket and gave it to me)

As soon as I touched the locket,

Anne wanted to see who was the person who killed her daughter and her.

CHAPTER TWENTY-THREE

THE FACE OF THE MURDERER

It was time to see who murdered ruby and her mother.

Anne asked me to hand over the locket to her.

I handed it over, and she spoke some spells holding the locket in her hands, and asked me to touch the locket.

As soon as I touched the locket, the murderer's face was revealed. I was shocked to see it was my dad.

Anne screamed This guy killed my daughter now, she will kill my father.

I said how come this is possible my mother said, my father died in an accident how come she could kill your daughter?

She replied your father is alive, your mother fibbed to you because he finagled on her. I was crying after listening to this. Now, I despised my father I wanted to kill him.

CHAPTER TWENTY-FOUR

KILLING MY FATHER

I took the enchanted knife and asked Anne where I could find him. She replied you have to ask the locket for this. I asked if the locket showed a house.

Anne said we could teleport there but your buddies can not go. They are normal humans and they will reach their residence automatically.

I replied what do you mean by that? I am not an ordinary human?

She said no, you are a special person. Let's go and kill the person who killed my lovely daughter ruby.

(We teleported to my father's house.)

I was holding the enchanted knife in my hands.

We went to the room where my father was sitting.

My father was surprised to see me and Anne in his house.)

Anne asked him why he killed ruby. Now, she would kill me.

I was astounded to hear what Anne said. I asked her Why she used me? I wanted to help her.

My father said the death of ruby was a misfortune, please don't kill my son.

She took the magical knife from my hands and chortled loudly.

My father shrieked noo don't kill him if you want to kill someone kill me.

She stabbed the knife into my abdomen and suddenly I heard something wake up!

CHAPTER TWENTY-FIVE

DREAM!

My vision opened and my mother was in front of me. I was on my mattress.

My mother was shouting at me to wake up!

I realized what all just happened was just a dream! I asked my mother where my father was. she replied he was in his headquarters and asked me what happened.

I replied nothing.

Ginny came and said to me lethargic. I was angry at her.

I called my buddies and asked if they were okay. They replied what will happen to us? We are alright. Did anything happen?

I said nothing, I just wanted to know if they were fine. I said bye.

CHAPTER TWENTY-SIX

WAS IT A DREAM OR NOT?

At night after dinner I went to watch television with Ginny for a while after that I remembered I forgot something in the store room.

(In the store room.)

I was not able to find my lost thing but I found a crystal ball.

Maybe, Anne, Ruby was not a dream!

End

Thank you for reading this book. more books coming soon.

33